FRANZ was always meddling. You couldn't leave him alone for a minute without him poking his nose in this or his fingers in that. And wild? As wild as the wind he was, and reckless, getting himself into one terrible fix after another.

Finally, his father told him, "Mend your ways or leave this house!"

Well, Franz tried his best to mend his ways but it wasn't long before he poked his nose in this again and his fingers in that and got himself in another terrible fix and before he knew it he was on the street with nothing but a clipped ear and his clothes tied up in a bundle.

Ye Liste of
Apprenticeships

As it happened, it was the time of year when tradespeople were taking on new apprentices. You could learn to bake bread, make sausages or cheeses. You could do carpentry or masonry, tailoring, shoemaking. There were all kinds of useful, steady jobs to be had. But Franz wanted none of them. Oh, no! He wanted something much more exciting, something spectacular and grand. So he set off for the city where he thought he might find such a job.

Franz found himself in a strange part of the country. By and by, he came to an old gateway – a very peculiar old gateway, with a pair of snarling dragons on the pillars. Beneath one of them was a notice which read

APPRENTICE WANTED – APPLY WITHIN

Franz wondered what sort of apprenticeship it might be. He ventured up the path, finding nothing but a tangle of creepers and vines. Then, and this was very odd, for the sky was as blue as a periwinkle, he heard a low rumble of thunder. He ventured a little further, picking his way through the undergrowth. With every step the thunder grew louder, and there was another sound, like the cracking of whips. Suddenly he came to a clearing – Franz could hardly believe what he saw through the trees.

Soaring up in a jagged confusion of towers and turrets was a castle. Dark clouds swirled above it, and on one of its ramparts stood a man. He was wielding a staff. Lightning sprang from its tip, ripping through the clouds with mighty cracks, whipping them to a frenzy of thunderclaps.

That's the job for me, thought Franz, and climbed up to the castle.

By the front door, under the bell, was the name

LUDVIG
HEXENMEISTER
SORCERER

Franz seized the bell-rope and pulled.

The thunder died away. In its place a booming of doors being opened and shut echoed down through the castle until the front door swung open and the sorcerer appeared.

"This way," he said.

Franz followed him to a vast laboratory, so filled with curious-looking apparatus that his fingers twitched in his pockets.

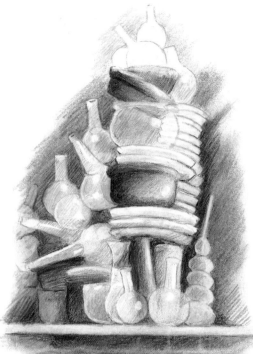

"Your task," said the sorcerer, pointing to a sink, "will be the washing-up. It is to be done first thing each morning without fail."

Franz gaped at the huge pile of glassware teetering on the draining board.

But that wasn't the worst of it – not by any means!

For beside the sink was a hearth in which hung a big black cauldron. It was for heating the water he would need – water he must draw from a river at the bottom of a deep ravine.

The sorcerer showed Franz a flight of steps so steep they seemed to disappear into the abyss. Down, down he went, endlessly down. Long before he reached the bottom he heard the torrent racing below. He charged his buckets and carried them up to fill the cauldron. But did they fill it? No. Not even half-way. Poor Franz! Twice he had to go back for more, struggling up the steps until his legs felt like jelly and his head spun.

Rain or shine, fair weather or foul, at the crack of dawn Franz fetched the water and washed up while the sorcerer snored in his bed. Later, he was free to watch him at his work.

There seemed no limit to the amazing things his new master could do. He made chairs dance polkas, tables fly round rooms, horses prance where, before, there were mere wisps of manes and tails. A handful of feathers he could turn into a flock of squawking birds. Not a week went by, hardly a day, when Franz did not see him cast some new spell, each one more astonishing than the last.

But there was a particular spell the sorcerer used over and over again: to charm an old broom and put it to work. Still weary from his arduous task, Franz would watch enviously as the broom stood up, grew arms and did various odd jobs at the sorcerer's bidding. And all this spell consisted of was the briefest of rhymes and a simple potion.

Franz had seen the sorcerer mix this potion many times. It looked so easy, he felt sure that he could do it too. Of course the sorcerer wouldn't hear of it.

"Remember the rule," he told Franz severely. "Observe, learn, but *do not touch.*"

Franz thrust his hands deep into his pockets. But the twitching of his meddlesome fingers increased with each passing day.

Then one morning the sorcerer was called away. It was the opportunity Franz had been waiting for.

The instant the coast was clear, Franz got to work. But what had looked so easy in the hands of the sorcerer, for Franz proved very difficult indeed.

First he ground the pink powder with the blue, then the yellow with the white. Yet when he stirred them into the orange liquid, it didn't turn purple as it should. Again he ground the powders. Still the liquid refused to change colour. However many times Franz tried, he couldn't get the quantities quite right. But did he give up? He did not! He was determined to mix this potion. For without it he could not bewitch the broom. And Franz meant to make the broom his servant, to have it work for him as it did for the sorcerer. He would send it into the ravine to fetch the water in the mornings and then have it wash up for him while he, Franz, its master, went back to bed.

He worked on patiently, doggedly, never wavering from his purpose until, at last, the liquid shivered in its flask. Slowly it took on a vivid violet hue. Franz marvelled at the way it glittered with tiny sparks. He had done it. He had mixed the magic potion!

He ran to fetch the broom.

Franz sprinkled the potion on to its handle and began to chant.

"Old servant, now's the time,
To feel the power of my rhyme;
Dreamless slumbering forsake,
Thy master calls thee, slave. AWAKE!"

The broom shook itself like a dog. It sprouted two arms and stood up on its bristles.

"Draw the water," Franz commanded. "Pour it in that ancient cauldron of blackened tin."

The broom seized the buckets and off it marched – through the door and down the endless flights of steps to the river at the bottom of the ravine.

In no time at all, the broom returned, lurching in, water slapping in its buckets. Franz watched with satisfaction as it began to fill the cauldron. Then off it went again to the abyss. Back it came, lurching and swaying. Splash, went the water into the cauldron. Away the broom went to fetch more. For the third time it returned, filling the cauldron to the brim.

Franz raised his hand in a signal to stop his tireless helper. He opened his mouth to give the command, but – oh, horror! He had forgotten the words. Try as he might he could not remember them!

The broom turned to go down to the river once more.

"Stop, broom!" Franz shouted.

But the broom ignored him.

"Stop! Stop! Please stop!" he cried, clutching at its handle.

But the broom was already out of the door.

Desperately Franz searched the sorcerer's books for the words he could not remember.

Too soon the broom returned, striding purposefully towards the cauldron. Franz tried to block its way but, like some mindless machine, it pushed past him. It emptied its buckets. The water overflowed and put out the fire.

Now the broom was no longer a helper. Now it seemed a demon, as it turned yet again and made for the door.

Franz had to stop it! He must not let it refill the buckets. He seized an axe and chopped the broom in two. It fell to the floor and lay there like a dead thing, still at last.

But not for long. The two halves began to quiver. Then up they rose! Two brooms, now, instead of one, with four buckets, strode through the door.

Franz panicked. He smashed the brooms to splinters, thinking to destroy them entirely.

He could not have been
more mistaken. There was a
whisper, a rustle, a shuffling
and a creaking. His eyes
widened with horror. His
hair stood on end. Each tiny
splinter had grown into
a broom. Each broom had
two buckets. An army of
brooms and buckets were
marching out of the door!

Franz was powerless to stop them. There was nothing he could do. The rattle of a thousand buckets receded into the ravine. Then, hideously, terrifyingly, it rose again. In a hellish procession, the brooms came clanking back to empty their buckets into the streaming cauldron. Water lapped against the walls and surged round the table legs, growing deeper as the brooms went back again and again to fill their buckets, swarming like fiends down the steps to the river.

It was like a horrible nightmare. If he ever got out of it he would never meddle again.

"Old servant, thy labours cease,
Lest this maelstrom increase.
Thy hellish trickery is done,
From wood and bristle, sprite, BEGONE! "

Franz heard the sorcerer's words ring
out over the chaos. For a second all
was still. Then suddenly, the water
whirled into an angry, hissing spout.
With a loud sucking and gurgling, as
if the plug had been pulled from a
giant bathtub, it vanished.

There wasn't a trace of it left, not a
puddle. The broom, too, was back in its
corner, its demonic counterparts gone.
Only Franz's tell-tale mess remained.

"Hmm," said the sorcerer, studying the
remains of the purple potion and swilling it
round in its flask.

Franz shifted guiltily from foot to foot.
"Boy..."

I'm done for, Franz thought.

"You have the makings of a sorcerer!"

Franz looked up, not believing his ears.

"Do not, however, suppose," the sorcerer
continued, "that there will be no penalty for
your crime, for crime it is to meddle in
things you do not understand. I trust you
have learnt your lesson?"

Franz had indeed learnt his lesson! From that day on, he worked diligently, heeding the sorcerer's every word. And one day – long, long, long afterwards – it was Franz who stood on the ramparts of the castle, wielding a staff from which lightning sprang, whipping the clouds into a frenzy of thunderclaps.